Pastry School in Paris

An Adventure in Capacity

Cindy Neuschwander

illustrated by Bryan Langdo

Henry Holt and Company

New York

For my mom, Carol Grazda—
Our trip to Paris was such fun! —C. N.

For my kitchen assistant, Oliver —B. L.

Special thanks to the California Culinary Academy
for allowing me to observe baking in action,
and to Christine Farlin, who helped me with French words

Henry Holt and Company, LLC
Publishers since 1866
175 Fifth Avenue
New York, New York 10010
mackids.com

Library of Congress Cataloging-in-Publication Data
Neuschwander, Cindy.
Pastry school in Paris : an adventure in capacity / Cindy Neuschwander ; illustrated by Bryan Langdo.—1st ed.
p.   cm.
Summary: Twins Bibi and Matt learn about different liquid measurements when they go to
Les Jumelles Coccinelle International Pastry Academy while on a trip to Paris with their parents and dog.
ISBN 978-0-8050-8314-9
[1. Cookery—Fiction. 2. Volume (Cubic content)—Fiction. 3. Liquids—Measurement—Fiction. 4. Twins—Fiction.
5. Brothers and sisters—Fiction. 6. Paris—Fiction.] I. Langdo, Bryan, ill. II. Title.
PZ7.N4453Pas 2009   [E]—dc22   2008013425

First Edition—2009
The artist used Winsor & Newton watercolors on Aquarelle Arches paper to create the illustrations for this book.
Printed in China by RR Donnelley Asia Printing Solutions Ltd., Dongguan City, Guangdong Province.

3 5 7 9 10 8 6 4

"These brownies are delicious!" Matt and Bibi's mother took another bite.

"We made them ourselves," the twins said proudly.

"Your baking shows real talent," said their father. "When we go to Paris, let's visit a cooking school. Maybe you can learn to make other tasty desserts."

"Paris? Oo la la!" sang Bibi. She danced around the kitchen.

"Have apron, will travel!" chimed in Matt.

A few weeks later the
Zills family arrived in Paris
and took a whirlwind
tour of the city.

Then they went to Les Jumelles Coccinelle International Pastry Academy. Celine Coccinelle was the head chef and her twin, Marie, ran the school's café.

Matt looked at the school's sign. "Wow!" he said, pointing up. "How do you say that?"

"It's pronounced *lay jhoo-mel cox-ee-nel,*" answered his mom.

While Riley chased butterflies in the tiny back garden, everyone in the class put on aprons and practiced mixing cake batters.

"Man!" said Matt. "Baking is hard work! I'm thirsty."

"How about a cold drink?" asked Bibi, opening a refrigerator
that was full of drinks from around the world. She handed Matt
a short, round bottle and chose a tall, slender one for herself.

"Hey! No fair!" he protested. "You get more than I do!"

Bibi looked at both labels. "No," she said. "They each contain
one pint."

"How much is that?" asked Matt, gulping thirstily.

Bibi shrugged. "I'm not sure."

Chef Celine clapped her hands, and the students gathered around her. "You are now ready to begin dessert making," she said. "Measuring ingredients exactly is *very* important. Please read your recipes carefully."

Everyone in the class was given a special job. The twins were in charge of liquids.

"Matt and Bibi," said Chef Celine. "For cooking, liquids are often measured in parts of quarts or liters." She pointed to red and blue lines on the side of a large measuring cup. "Here's a chart to help you." Then she hurried away to rescue a sinking soufflé.

Matt and Bibi looked at the paper. It read:

AMERICAN MEASUREMENTS

1 pint = 2 cups
1 quart = 4 cups
1 half gallon = 8 cups
1 gallon = 16 cups

FRENCH MEASUREMENT

1 liter = 1,000 milliliters

"Let's try testing it," suggested Bibi.

They filled Matt's empty bottle with water and poured it into the measuring cup.

"One pint *is* the same as two cups," she said, looking at the partly filled container.

Suddenly Chef Celine called out, "Matt! Bibi! We need a quart of water over here at the stove. We're making lollipops! We can use them later to decorate our cakes."

Matt added more water to the measuring cup. Bibi carried it across the kitchen and emptied it into a saucepan that had a sugar mixture in it.

Another student stirred. Soon the pot began to boil.

"Now a little peppermint oil for flavor," said Chef Celine, handing Bibi a small bottle. "But too much will make it smell like a toothpaste factory!" she warned.

Plink, plink, plink. Bibi squeezed a milliliter into the mix. Then the hot liquid was poured into molds to harden. But it didn't.

"I think we have lollipop soup!" said Chef Celine. "Perhaps there was too much water in the pan."

Matt looked at the measuring cup. "Oh, no!" he exclaimed. "I must have used one liter of water instead of one quart. A liter is more than a quart. No wonder it's runny!"

Cooking school was fun, but it was also tiring. After a few days in the kitchen, Chef Celine told the class, "Tomorrow we'll have a day off. I've arranged a trip to the Eiffel Tower."

Everyone gathered at the bus stop the next morning. When the bus arrived, the class began climbing on. Matt, Bibi, and Riley were the last in line.

"No big dogs allowed!" snapped the driver. The twins and
their pet jumped back and the doors slammed shut.

"We're taking Riley back," Bibi called to her parents as the
bus pulled away.

The twins met Marie running toward the bus stop.

"Help! Help!" she cried.

"What's the matter?" asked Bibi.

"The Inspector General of French cooking schools will be here in just two hours! He'll expect our finest dessert! Anything less and we'll earn a poor grade."

"We'll stay and help you," Matt offered.

"I cannot cook!" wailed Marie.

"Then Bibi and I will make the dessert," he announced.

"Celine keeps special recipes in her desk," said Marie helpfully. Today there was just one in the drawer. She handed it to Bibi, who read it aloud:

> Four cups is what it takes.
> One quart is what it makes.
> One half is milk, one half is cream.
> Whip in egg yolks; heat to steam.
> Mix in sugar, one whole cup.
> Vanilla bean will spice it up.
> Bake cherry cake. Churn, mold, and chill.
> Voilà! Serve up this icy thrill!

"Oh dear," said Marie. "That sounds like an ice cream cake!"

"No worries," said Matt, tying on an apron. "They don't call me the Cake King for nothing!"

Marie smiled. "I'll set a table for the Inspector General," she said, bustling off.

"Now what?" asked Bibi.

Matt looked at the clock. "We don't have time to make that fancy cake," he said. "Let's bake brownies instead."

"And we could put the ice cream on top for a truly yummy dessert!" added his sister.

The twins hurried out to buy what they needed for their brownie recipe. When they returned they mixed the ingredients and put the pan of batter into the oven to bake. But they had never made ice cream before.

"First we have to figure out this recipe," said Bibi. "One half is milk and one half is cream?"

"Let's start with a half *cup* of each," suggested Matt.

"Okay," agreed Bibi, measuring out both into a pan.

Then they whipped in the yolks. As this cooked, it burbled, boiled, and lumped.

"Eewww! It looks like rotten scrambled eggs!" said Bibi.

BRRRRING! The oven timer rang, and Matt pulled out the brownies.

Marie poked her head into the kitchen. "The Inspector
General will be here in less than an hour," she announced.
"Mmmm! It smells sweet and chocolaty in here!"

"Thanks!" replied Bibi, quickly dumping their eggy disaster
in the garbage.

As soon as Marie left, Matt said, "We can't freeze up now!
We've got ice cream to make."

The twins looked at Chef Celine's directions again.

"This recipe takes four cups, so let's try two cups of milk and two cups of cream," said Bibi.

Together they scanned their chart.

"Two cups is a pint," observed Matt. "Why didn't Chef Celine just write 'pint' in the recipe? Measuring liquids can get confusing."

Bibi agreed. "Yeah, and two pints is the same as four cups, which equals one quart. Some measurements have more than one name. Let's go, go, go!"

"RRRROOOFF!" agreed Riley.

"This has now become a three-chef job," said Matt, eyeing Riley. "And you have just the muscle power we need." He attached a whisk to his dog's wagging tail and placed a bowl of yolks on a stool. "Whip away!" Matt told him. Egg foam flew everywhere.

While Matt combined the other ingredients, Bibi got the ice cream maker ready. Then they poured everything into it and turned it on.

Bibi started tidying up. "Matt!" she cried. "Did you add *that* to the ice cream!" She pointed to an open container.

"I did," said Matt proudly. "We almost overlooked the crushed vanilla bean. I also threw in a few cherries."

"*This,*" said Bibi, tapping another jar, "is the vanilla! You just put in pepper!"

"Wow! This ice cream will be red hot!" said Matt. He peeked
out the window. Marie was seating the Inspector General.
"Maybe he won't notice."

Bibi placed a piece of brownie on a plate, put two small scoops of the freshly made cherry-pepper ice cream on top, and decorated it with mint leaves from the garden.

"At least it looks nice," said Matt.

Bibi smiled faintly and together they took the plate out to the Inspector General.

"Hmmm," he said, looking at them sternly. "What is this?"

Bibi thought quickly. "It's called Ladybugs in the Garden," she replied.

The Inspector General leaned forward and sniffed. He took a bite. There was a moment of silence and . . .

"Magnifique!" he cheered, slapping his hand on the table.
"The pepper! It adds such *ZING!*"

Matt grinned at his sister. "I guess he did notice."

"Let's go clean up the kitchen and Riley," Bibi said.

"One squirt of liquid soap mixed with sixteen cups of water
will give us a gallon of suds," said Matt. "That should do the job!"

A Note to Teachers and Parents

Capacity (the amount a container can hold) is both familiar and foreign to young children. They may understand the concept of a cup from informal cooking experiences, but they can become confused with such terms as pint and liter. In *Pastry School in Paris*, Chef Celine uses both American standard and metric measurements for baking.

Here are some ideas you can try for more fun with capacity:

- Find two bottles with different shapes but the same capacities. Have a child predict if one will hold more, and if one will hold less. Then fill each one with the same amount of liquid. Young children often think that tall containers hold more than short ones.

- Mix enough water with food coloring to fill both a quart bottle and a liter bottle. Then have your child compare the two bottles.

- Include children in actual cooking experiences. Like Matt and Bibi, let youngsters be in charge of liquid measurements. This will help them to see practical applications for capacities.

- Liquids can be measured in very small amounts. Have a child see how many teaspoons equal a tablespoon and how many tablespoons equal a cup. Using an eyedropper, as Bibi did in the story, can help children measure milliliters.

- Collect 2 one-cup containers, 2 one-pint containers, 2 one-quart containers, 2 half-gallon containers, and 1 one-gallon jug. You and a child can test to see if two of one size container fill up the next biggest carton. This can help a child learn about liquid equivalencies.

- Help children practice converting from one capacity to another. Understanding that 4 cups = 2 pints = 1 quart takes practice. Find the different names for any one capacity.

- Encourage children to read labels on containers. This will help them understand how much liquid various bottles and containers actually hold.

Whatever activities you try, you can help children enjoy the math!